HUBBLE*BUBBLE

The WACKY WINTER WONDERLAND!

TRACEY CORDEROY

illustrated by JOE BERGER

nosy crow

An imprint of Candlewick Press

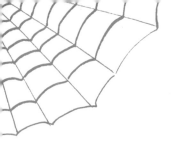

First U.S. edition 2017

Library of Congress Catalog Card Number pending
ISBN 978-0-7636-9624-5 (hardcover)
ISBN 978-0-7636-9625-2 (paperback)

17 18 19 20 21 22 BVG 10 9 8 7 6 5 4 3 2 1

Printed in Berryville, VA, U.S.A.

This book was typeset in Baskerville MT.
The illustrations were done in pen and ink and colored digitally.

Nosy Crow
an imprint of
Candlewick Press
99 Dover Street
Somerville, Massachusetts 02144

www.nosycrow.com
www.candlewick.com

For Kirsty and everyone
at Nosy Crow, thanks
for your support! x
T. C.

For Charlotte, Matilda,
Bea, Martha, Sybil, and
Spooky, with love. x
J. B.

CONTENTS

The
WACKY WINTER
WONDERLAND!

Chapter One

"Oooh, Granny!" Pandora cried. "Can I try one of your cookies?"

"Of course!" said Granny. "But wait a moment and I'll frost them!"

It was Christmas Eve and Granny was at Pandora's house doing Christmassy things. Pandora had just made a snowflake paper chain, while Granny had baked gingerbread snowmen.

Granny waved her wand and with a small **pop!** the cookies were all beautifully frosted.

She then took some small glass jars
filled with sweets and sprinkles from her
cauldron.

"These are *magical* sweets," Granny
said, giving each little snowman a row of
gumdrop buttons and a black licorice
top hat.

"*How* are they magical?" Pandora asked.

Granny just winked. "You'll see!"

With that, Pandora's parents, Hugo and
Moonbeam, arrived home. They'd been
out doing last-minute Christmas shopping.

"Mmmm—*gingerbread*!" Pandora's dad
said.

"My favorite!" agreed her mom.

Granny offered them the magical cookies, and they each took a bite. Pandora watched to see what would happen next. . . .

"Oh!" said her dad as he started to chew. "Those gumdrops are fizzing on my tongue!"

"Mine too!" Her mom giggled. "So tickly!"

They both swallowed. And then, in a puff of magic snowflakes, Pandora's dad turned into a *snowman*! By his side was a snow-woman wearing a headband of snowdrops . . . and a frown.

Pandora gasped. "Mom? Dad?"

"Surprise!" called Granny. "*That's* what the magic sweets do!"

Pandora looked worried.

"It's all right," Granny said. "It was just a bit of fun. Watch this!"

With a flick of her wand,
the snow melted away to
reveal Pandora's parents
underneath it.

They were wet. And they
didn't look happy with Granny
at all.

"No more M-A-G-I-C!"
puffed Hugo, dripping onto
the carpet.

"Not for the rest of the
day," Moonbeam added icily.
She sighed. "Now, isn't it time
you were going?"

"Good heavens!" said
Granny, checking the clock.
"You're right!"

11

Granny was taking Pandora to a nearby farm that had been turned into a Winter Wonderland. There was going to be a sparkly ice rink, jolly elves, and yummy Christmas food. There was even a magical sleigh ride to see Santa!

Pandora clapped her hands.

"Hooray!" she cheered. She'd been looking forward to this for ages!

Granny whistled for her broomstick, and they both jumped on.

"Full speed ahead!" cried Pandora.

Chapter Two

But when they arrived at the Winter Wonderland, Pandora's face fell.

The thin, patchy snow smelled like shaving foam, the farmyard was dotted with horse poop, and the farmer selling tickets looked really *angry*.

"That cat can't come in, for starters!" he huffed, glowering at Cobweb.

"But it's a *farm*," replied Granny.

"Well!" said the farmer. "You'll need to buy a ticket for him, too!"

Granny paid, and they marched away to explore. There were crowds of people, but they all looked glum. This place was really horrible.

The shaving-foam snow was all sticky and gross. And it made poor Cobweb sneeze!

And the ice rink wasn't *real* ice either—
just dirty sheets of bubble wrap stuck
together.

"Want to skate?" growled a grumpy-looking elf, waving a pair of grubby ice skates.

16

"Hang on," said Pandora. It was Rory, a fifth-grader from her school. His friend Ben stood beside him in a hat with a bell, scowling. "You're not elves!" Pandora said.

"Are so!" Rory spat. Then he lowered his voice so Granny couldn't hear. "And say that again and we'll tell Santa you've been bad!"

"And you know what that will mean." Ben glared. "No presents!"

With that, Pandora spied Nellie and Jake standing outside the Festive Food Hall with Jake's dad. She hurried Granny over, happy to see her friends.

The Festive Food Hall was just a damp old tent. The "festive food" was disappointing, too.

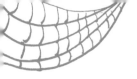

"Want my sprouts?" asked Jake.

"No, thanks!" Pandora said with a shudder.

"How about my mug of cold tea?" asked Nellie, sighing.

With that, Farmer Grumpypants appeared, leading Santa's "reindeer" through the yard.

"Those aren't reindeer!" grumbled Jake. "They're *dogs* with antlers on their heads!"

Pandora sighed. "I wish they *were* reindeer."

"Maybe they can be?" whispered Granny, slipping out her wand.

"Better not," said Pandora. "The farmer might get even madder."

They watched as the dogs were led into a barn where a pig trough on wheels stood waiting.

"Oh, no!" gasped Pandora. "Is *that* the sleigh that takes you on the magical ride to Santa?"

She looked at Granny, almost in tears. But Granny's eyes were twinkling. And as soon as the farmer closed the barn door behind him, Granny flicked her wand at the fake ice rink and it turned into a real one instead! With another quick wand flick, the children's poop-splattered boots became the *sparkliest* ice skates.

"Even Cobweb's got some!" Pandora giggled as Granny launched him onto the ice.

"Wheeee!"

Chapter Three

Ice-skating was great!

Pandora went slowly, but Granny leaped and spun. *"Beep beep!"* she called as she weaved through the crowds. "Such fun!"

After their skating, everyone was hungry, so Granny magicked up some *real* festive food. Gone were the mugs of stone-cold tea. Instead they had yummy hot chocolate

with marshmallows, and cupcakes
decorated like reindeer.

"*Mmmm,*" said the children,
digging in. "Thanks, Granny!"

When it got dark, they trekked
across the fields to see the
Twinkling Tunnel of Lights.
But they shouldn't have bothered,
because when they got there . . .

The Twinkling Tunnel was just two bare trees with some lightbulbs strung between them.

"*Oh, no!*" the children exclaimed.

"*Really!*" spluttered Granny. "Leave this to me!" She pointed her wand at the trees and shouted:

"Out with winter trees so bare—and in with

TWINKLES

everywhere!"

Whoosh—a stream of sparkles burst from her wand and hit the bare trees full force. All at once they began sprouting big green leaves.

Then, climbing roses sprang from the earth, curling up the tree trunks and arching over to make the most *magical* tunnel.

"And look!" cried Pandora as hundreds of fairy lights twinkled among the roses.

Suddenly, a little cluster of lights *flew off*.
Pandora looked more closely.

The fairy lights weren't *lights* at all, but
real *fairies* with rainbow-colored wings!

More and more fairies fluttered off to
play. Some were graceful, while others were
little acrobats. And one bunch was really
quite spirited. . . .

"Wheee!" They showered the children in petals they'd just tugged off the bushes. Then one naughty fairy snatched Granny's wand and zoomed out of reach. "Hee-hee!"

"Hey! No!" cried Granny. "Give me back my wand!" But the fairy just stuck her tongue out at her!

She flicked Granny's wand — and to the fairy's delight, magic *snowflakes* puffed out of the end.

"Oooooooh!" said the fairy, and she flicked the wand again.

And again,
and again,
and again!

In no time all, a small blizzard was raging as everyone dived for the wand.

Then all of a sudden Jake yelled, *"Someone's coming!"* and everyone peered through the snowstorm.

"Oh, no!" Pandora gave a little squeak. "It's Farmer Grumpypants!"

Chapter Four

"Who's snowing in my field?" the farmer roared, battling through the magical storm.

Gasping, the fairy dropped the wand and Granny snatched it up.

"Quick, everyone!" she cried as the farmer got closer. "Follow me!"

Turning, Granny raced off through the field, and everyone dashed behind.

As they ran, Nellie saw that the magical snow had stopped, but the sky was still filled with fluffy white things.

"Look, Pandora!" she called, and Pandora looked up.

"It's *really* snowing!"

They followed Granny through the
snow-covered fields, but the farmer was
catching up.

"Aha!" said Granny. She knew *just* the
thing. With a flick of her wand, they were
all wearing skis. "He'll never catch us
now!" she said.

The wind whistled through their hair as they skied uphill and down. They flew past the ice rink, which glistened in the dark. The smell of hot chocolate still hung in the air, and the trees were all fluffy with snow.

"It looks *so* pretty now!" Pandora said.

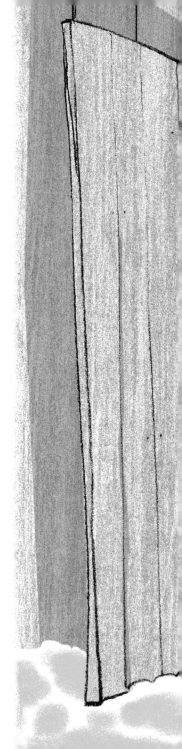

Granny then led them across the farmyard, where any stray horse poop was now buried deep beneath a thick blanket of snow.

"In here!" she cried, pulling open the big barn door.

Inside, the "reindeer" were all snoozing. But their eyes opened wide at the sight of Granny, and their ears pricked up at once.

"Ah, yes," said Granny as their tails started wagging. "You're ready for an adventure. Me, too!"

She waved her wand and— **whizz-pop!**—the old pig trough turned into the most *beautiful* sleigh, decorated with holly, ivy, and red-and-white candy canes.

Granny put harnesses on the dogs, who looked very excited. Then she hurried everyone into the sleigh and quickly took up the reins.

"But those reindeer are *dogs*," said Nellie. "They can't *fly*!"

"They can now!" said Pandora. She waved her wand at the dogs.

"Take us on a magical sleigh ride!" she called. "Izzy-wizzy-otious!"

Pandora's spell did the trick beautifully. The dogs trotted out through the open door, and the sleigh slowly lifted off the ground.

But the farmer was coming through the yard. "Oh, no you don't!" he called at them, waving Granny's broomstick in the air.

"Oh, yes we do!" Granny yelled back with a grin. And as the sleigh whooshed over his head, she leaned out and grabbed her broomstick.

"Merry Christmas!" she cried as they zoomed away—up, and up, and up!

Pandora had never had such a *magical*
ride. Not even on Granny's broomstick!
Soon they were soaring past a huge silver
moon, looking down on beautiful snowy
rooftops.

Pandora snuggled up with her friends. As *Winter Wonderlands* went, this had to be the most wacky and *wonderful* EVER!

BEST
IN
SHOW!

Chapter One

Pandora was at Granny's house, getting Cobweb ready for a pet show at the Town Hall. All the pets had to look their very best *and* have a special talent. Cobweb was nervously waiting for his bath.

"Now, which bubble bath shall we use?" asked Granny.

"Um . . ." said Pandora.

Granny's bathroom was full of special lotions and potions.

"Aha!" said Granny, picking up a bottle. "Cotton Candy Surprise! Perfect!"

Granny poured the red potion into Cobweb's bathwater. The water fizzed, then turned bright pink.

Carefully, Granny lowered Cobweb in, and Pandora started to wash him. When he was clean, they rinsed off the bubbles, and then Granny dried him with her hair dryer.

All was going well, until suddenly — doingggggg! Cobweb's silky gray fur had turned shocking pink and fluffed out like cotton candy!

"Arggh!" shrieked Granny. "Silly me! I forgot—Cotton Candy Surprise sometimes does that."

"But how can we fix it?" Pandora cried. "He can't enter the pet show like *that*!"

Granny thought for a moment. Then she waved her wand over Cobweb's fluffed-out fur. With a magical pop! the pink fuzziness vanished, and Cobweb was back to normal.

"And look!" said Pandora. She had found a black-currant-smelling pamper mitt.

49

Pandora sat Cobweb beside her on the sofa and rubbed the mitt softly down his back.

"Goodness!" said Granny. It made his fur shine like the sun.

Cobweb's special talent was tightrope walking and trapeze. Granny had rigged up a tightrope in the yard and a trapeze swing hanging off the tree. They took Cobweb out for one last practice before they had to head to the show.

"That's the way, Cobweb!" Pandora yelled as the little gray cat glided across the tightrope without a wiggle or wobble in sight. "I think he might even win the show."

"We should *get* him there, then!" Granny said, looking at her watch. She whistled for her broomstick.

"Off we go!"

Chapter
Two

The sidewalk outside the Town Hall was already crowded with talented pets when Pandora and Granny got in line.

Pandora sized up the competition. There was a dancing dog, a sliding snail, and even a singing goldfish!

"He can sing *opera*," his owner boasted to Pandora.

Granny looked worried. "These pets are really talented."

"Well, Cobweb is talented, too!"
Pandora said with a smile.

They all went inside, gave details about
their pets, and lined them up for Round
One. This round was called Bright Eyes
and Bushy Tails! The judges were
looking for well-groomed, healthy-looking
pets.

Two judges walked along the line, examining each pet in turn. One of them reminded Pandora of a stick insect—he was so tall and thin. And the other (who looked like a pug) was saying such *snippy* things.

"I don't like the look of your goldfish's poop!"

"That dog has mud on its nose."

"Eww—your snail is leaving slime trails *everywhere*!"

Finally, they stopped at Cobweb, who was sitting in Granny's arms. Cobweb's gray coat looked as soft as velvet.

"So *shiny*." The thin judge nodded.

Granny nudged Pandora and gave a little wink. "As shiny as a black currant!" she whispered. "Thanks to you!"

The lady judge checked Cobweb's eyes. Then his ears, nose, and tail.

"A nice long tail," she said, and Granny
beamed.

The judges wrote a few things down,
then moved down the line. When the pets
had all been checked, the judges went out
to award their points in private. When they
came back, Round Two would begin. This
round, called Clever Creatures, was where
the pets would show off their special talents.

While everyone waited for the judges to come back, Granny magicked up a tightrope for Cobweb to walk across later. Then she joined all the other contestants for a drink.

Cobweb had a big saucer of milk
while Granny and Pandora both chose
milk shakes. Granny used her wand to give
them extra froth and sprinkles! Pandora
was just finishing hers off when a little
boy behind her
yelled, "MOM!"

His guinea pig had wandered into
another pet's carrying case, and somehow
the door had jammed shut.

"Open the door!" the little boy shouted.
"MOM!"

His mother dashed over and gave the
door a tug, but it wouldn't budge an inch.

"Yoo-hoo!" said Granny with a wave.
"Maybe *I* could help?"

She jumped to her feet, her wand in the
air. "Stand back!"

Chapter Three

"Granny—no—stop!" Pandora gasped. "Unjamming spells are so tricky!"

"Not for me, dear!" Granny insisted. "Watch this!"

She tapped the case door with her wand and uttered the spell *"Open-up-i-o!"*

The door gave a twitch, but stayed firmly shut.

"Hmm," said Granny. "This calls for more *powerful* magic!"

Taking a step back, she rolled up her sleeves, a determined twinkle in her eyes.

Pandora had seen that look before. It *always* appeared right before Granny went a bit too far.

"Wait!" cried Pandora. "We'll *both* try pulling the door!"

"Don't worry, dear!" Granny replied. "Trust me!"

Pandora could hardly bear to look as Granny waved her wand in huge circles. Magic swirls began shooting off *everywhere* and spinning around the room. . . .

Ping!
Ping!
Ping!—they hit the carrying case, and
the door sprang open at once.

"There—you see!" Granny said with a
smile.

"But look!" gasped Pandora. The magical
swirls were pinging off the *pets* now, too!

"Um—don't worry!" said Granny,
looking worried. "I . . . oooo . . ."

With that, the swirls faded and vanished
from sight. And for a moment all seemed
well. Then a teeny-tiny kitten opened its
teeny-tiny mouth and . . .

"Woof!"

But that wasn't all. The donkey beside him then gave a tiny

"Meow!"

"Ribbit!"

croaked a bunny, just like a frog!

"Granny!" yelled Pandora. "Their voices are all muddled!" And their *talents* had been mixed up, too. . . .

The dog wasn't dancing anymore, but
sliding like the *snail* had been! And the snail
was perched on the rabbit's skateboard,
whizzing around the room like a rocket.

"Whoever heard of a *skateboarding snail*?"
his owner cried angrily.

"My granny didn't mean it," Pandora muttered. "Unjamming spells are *so* hard. And she *did* free the guinea pig who was stuck!"

"Yeah!" agreed the little boy. "But now look — he thinks he's a singing *goldfish*!"

He pointed to his guinea pig, who was singing opera at the top of his voice.

"Ombra mai fu di vegetabile!"

Pandora blushed. "He's singing it really well, though. . . ."

Quickly, Granny searched through her book for a spell to fix everything. But it was too late — the side door opened, and in came the judges for Round Two.

"Clever Creatures time!" the lady judge boomed.

"But —" began Granny. But the judges weren't listening.

"Line up those pets, please. Now!"

Chapter
Four

Pandora looked around for Cobweb as the
mixed-up pets were lined up.

"Where *is* he?" she said. Pandora
couldn't see him anywhere.

Meanwhile, Granny had found a spell
that would turn all the pets back to normal.
She waved her wand quickly, and with a
huge BANG! everything was back as it
should be.

"About time, too!" rumbled the snail's owner, still grumpy.

One by one, the pets performed and their special talents were judged. But still Pandora couldn't see Cobweb. *Had the magic swirls hit him and vanished him away?*

Then, just as the judges finished their scoring and were about to announce Best in Show, a little girl pointed to the ceiling and cried, *"Oooh — look!"*

Everyone looked up. There was Cobweb, three-quarters of the way across the tightrope.

Pandora held her breath, but he wasn't even wobbling. He was great!

69

Cobweb reached the end of the tightrope and bowed, and the judges smiled and nodded. They quickly scribbled something down on their clipboards. Then everyone gathered to find out who had won the show.

"Third," said the stick-insect judge, standing tall, "is Dexter the dancing dog!" Everyone clapped as Dexter tap-danced up for his ribbon.

"And second," he said, "is Holly
the hamster! A *very* nice roller-skating
performance!" Again, everyone clapped as
Holly got her frilly ribbon.

"And that just leaves first place!" said the
lady judge. "Best in Show goes to . . ."
She paused, and Pandora crossed her
fingers tightly.

"Cobweb the cat for his shiny coat and *amazing* tightrope walking and trapezing!"

As everyone clapped, Granny stepped forward with Cobweb in her arms. But suddenly someone was shouting over the applause.

"Hold on a minute!" It was the owner of Sparky, the sliding snail.

"*Trapezing,* did you say?" he asked. "I don't remember seeing any trapezing— he's a fake!"

"No, wait—he can trapeze!" Granny spluttered.

"Prove it or *lose* it!" cried someone else.

"OK!" said Granny. She put Cobweb down and jumped onto her broomstick with Pandora.

"Up, broom!" she cried. As it zoomed into the air, a trapeze tumbled down from the bristles, and Cobweb leaped up and caught it.

While Granny soared high above the crowd, Cobweb did the most *amazing* tricks. No one could say he couldn't trapeze after this!

As he flew past the judges, the cup was raised, and Cobweb scooped it up with his paw.

Then Granny looped-the-loop gracefully before heading to the open door.

"Even *superstars* need their supper!" she called back.

"Bye, then!" Pandora waved.

And clever old Cobweb trapezed ALL the way home!

MUSEUM MAYHEM!

Chapter One

All week at school, Pandora's class had been learning about different people from the past and how they lived. Now they were going to the museum in the evening to see the exhibits and stay for a special *sleepover*. It was what they'd all been waiting for!

The children and their teacher, Mr. Bibble, arrived at the museum just after supper. Granny had come along, too, as one of the chaperones.

The museum looked really spooky at night. Pandora and her friends couldn't wait to explore. Granny was excited, too. *Bringing History to Life* was the children's subject at school. And *nobody* could bring history to life like *she* could!

The class had been split into groups,

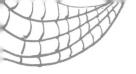

and each went off to a different area of the museum. Pandora's group went to see the Vikings first.

"Oh, a longboat!" Granny cried, immediately jumping into it. She waved her wand at some Viking figures sitting at the oars and bang!—they turned into a real Viking crew!

"Greetings!" roared the leader, Erik Bluetooth. "Ready for a voyage? We've got new *lands* to go and find!"

"Yay!" cheered the children. They couldn't miss a Viking adventure!

After climbing in, the children and
Granny joined the crew at the oars. Then
Granny flicked her wand at the floor, and a
huge, choppy ocean appeared.

"Look—we're wearing Viking *clothes*!"
cried Pandora. Even Cobweb the cat had
a mini Viking helmet with horns!

They set sail at once. The waves were
enormous.

"Awesome!" the children cried.

"But Granny," called Pandora as waves splattered her glasses and the longboat lurched and spun. "What if Mr. Bibble sees?"

"Then he can be a Viking, too, dear!" Granny said, and smiled.

On they went, until Jake spotted land. But before they could sail to it . . .

"Arggh!"

A museum attendant had opened the door — only to be met by an *ocean* gushing out into the corridor.

Before the attendant could step inside —
ping! — Pandora magicked the ocean away
and turned everything back to normal.
The attendant marched in. But by now
everyone was standing beside the longboat,
back in normal clothes.

He rubbed his eyes.

"Where did the *water* go? Oh, no — I
must be seeing things!"

Granny looked at Pandora, a puzzled
frown on her face.

"Why not tell him there *were* real
Vikings?" she whispered. After all, the trip
was all about bringing history to life!

"Um, w-where next?" Pandora whispered back. Granny checked her map, and her eyes lit up.

"To the Egyptians!" cried Granny, marching off. *"What fun!"*

Chapter Two

The moment they set foot in the Egyptian room, Granny waved her wand at an Egyptian sarcophagus and the door slowly opened with a *C-R-E-A-K*.

"Granny, what are you *doing*?" gasped Pandora. They'd been learning about sarcophagi at school. Inside them were mummies—dead Egyptian kings!

"Arggh!" screamed the children as the door opened wider. "Run!"

91

They scattered like ants and hid. Some dived into big stone urns; others darted behind statues. Pandora's friends dashed into a pyramid, but Pandora stayed put.

"Granny—um, bringing dead pharaohs to life is probably *not* a good idea."

"No," said Granny, giggling. "I just wanted a peek inside. I'll close it again if you like?"

Pandora nodded. "Yes, I think so. Um—*quick*!"

Granny waved her wand at the
sarcophagus, and — *C-R-E-A-K* —
the door closed again.

"Come out!" Pandora called to her friends.
"The coast is clear!"

Her friends crept out, and Pandora explained about the little mix-up. Then Granny magicked up some Egyptian paper and plant dyes, and some very special-looking pens.

"So, who'd like to try some Egyptian writing?" she asked.

"Yes, please!" cried the children. Hieroglyphics looked really fun.

As the children wrote, Granny turned herself into an Egyptian pharaoh. But an alive one, not a dead one, so that was OK.

Granny loved all the ancient jewelry she found lying around the exhibit. She liked wearing lots of thick black eye makeup, too.

When the children had finished their writing, they tried to work out one another's messages.

"No one will guess mine!"
Pandora said. She held up
her message and smiled.

"That's easy!" cried
Bluebell, who was great at
hieroglyphics. "That says—
I . . . love . . . my . . . squiggly
granny!"

"Not my *squiggly* granny!" Pandora said
with a smile. "Those squiggles are just for
decoration!"

"Well, I love you, too, dear!" Granny replied with a wink.

Now they were going to the Tudor room to meet up with the rest of their class. Granny magicked her normal(ish!) clothes back on and led everyone out.

"I can't wait for this!" Pandora cried. They'd been learning about the Tudors the week before.

"All those gowns—and even Henry the Eighth!" said Nellie.

This room would be the best one yet!

Chapter Three

But the Tudor room was dull—dull—
DULL!

There were only two figures, wearing
disappointing clothes. And on the Tudor
banqueting table were just three plastic
grapes and a pie.

Mr. Bibble explained that the Tudor
room was in the middle of a makeover.
"So lots of the things are missing,"
he said.

Pandora looked glum. "But Granny," she whispered, "there's not *even* a Henry the Eighth!"

"That doesn't mean there *can't* be one!" Granny grinned.

She turned to Mr. Bibble. "Don't you worry, dear—if you want history brought to life, I'm the one for the job! A *makeover*, you say? Why, I can do that in a jiffy!"

"I—I really don't think—" Mr. Bibble began. But it was too late.

Granny's wand was out
and suddenly— *TING!*—
all the children looked
like Tudors!

The girls' gowns were made from the softest silk, and the boys' doublets from the smoothest velvet. There were also knights, jesters, musicians with drums, and lutes and tambourines.

Pandora adored her pink silk gown. And as for Mr. Bibble, he slowly looked down to see a big round tummy!

Draped around his shoulders was a thick fur cape. On his head was a hat with a feather. And his trousers were gone, and in their place were . . .

"*Tights?!*" he squeaked. He looked at Granny. "Am I . . ."

"Yes, dear!" said Granny. "You're Henry the Eighth!"

"Tee-hee!" The children giggled. He looked so funny!

Now Granny waved her wand at the
plastic food, and a real Tudor banquet
appeared! There was roast goose with
cherries, jam tarts in the shape of shields,
and little Tudor roses made from cream.

"Hooray!" cried the children, digging in. And—wow—the food was so yummy! Why just *read* about a Tudor feast when you could eat one instead?

Finally, Mr. Bibble called everyone together. It was time to get ready for bed. The sleepover was happening in the Stone Age room, inside a big stone circle. As they walked over there, Granny magicked the children's Tudor outfits into Stone Age creature onesies instead.

"I'm not wearing one of those!" cried Mr. Bibble.

"Then you can stay as Henry!" Granny smiled. "But do stop being such a grouchy old grump . . . Your Highness!"

Chapter Four

They set up camp inside the stones under a figure of a big woolly mammoth. Nearby, a figure of a saber-toothed tiger bared its long, sharp teeth.

"This is so exciting!" the children exclaimed.

They wriggled into their sleeping bags, but they weren't tired. Neither was Granny.

"How about I magic up some playing cards?" she asked.

"No," said Mr. Bibble.

"Or some cocoa?"

"No!" Mr. Bibble sounded very firm. "One," he snapped, "my tights are too itchy! Two — you have done *enough* magic! And three — I'm tired. *Very* tired!"

"But we're not!" said the children.

"Too bad!"

Everyone silently settled back down. But *someone* was still feeling perky.

"How about we tell spooky stories?"
said Granny.

"Shhh!" hissed Mr. Bibble. "Sleep!"

Granny shook her head and sighed.
Sleepovers were meant to be fun!

"Granny! What are you *doing*?" whispered
Pandora as Granny drew out her wand.

"Bringing history to life again!" Granny
whispered back with a smile.

She pointed her wand at the saber-toothed tiger and gave it a secret little flick. The tiger blinked, then peered around the room, eyes wide.

"Granny," gasped Pandora, but Granny just winked.

"Don't worry, dear. He won't hurt anyone. The spell made him as gentle as a pussycat! Oh, and as *playful,* too—watch this."

They watched as the tiger spotted the feather on Mr. Bibble's "Henry" hat. The tiger twitched his tail, wiggled his bottom—then raced off to catch it!

"Rahh!" cried the tiger playfully as he bounded across the room. Mr. Bibble saw him coming.

"Argggh!" he screamed. He scrambled to his feet, then pounded to the door, his big round tummy wobbling.

"You can't eat *me*! I'm King Henry the Eighth, I'll have you know!"

Granny let out a giggle. "No, silly! He just wants to *play*—stop running!"

With that, the tiger leaped through the air and landed—*kerr-splatt!*—on Mr. Bibble.

He batted the feather with his paw. Then
out came his floppy wet tongue and—
SLUUUURRRPPPP!—he licked Mr. Bibble
on the nose!

"See?" said Granny, laughing. "He's just a *pussycat*!" And she tickled the tiger under his chin. "Coochie coo!"

The children were rolling around, laughing. Bringing history to life was such fun!

But everything was fun with a certain someone around. "Oh, Granny!" said Pandora. "You're the BEST!"